the VAMPIRE

The Tinned Poltergeist

CINAR

Television series © 1999 Fancy Cape Productions Inc.
a subsidiary of CINAR Corporation/Alphanim, France
3, Canal J. All rights reserved.

ORCHARD BOOKS
96 Leonard Street, London EC2A 4XD
Orchard Books Australia
32/45-51 Huntley Street, Alexandria, NSW 2015
ISBN 1 84362 814 7
First published in Great Britain in 1996
This edition published in 2004
Text © Hiawyn Oram 1996
Illustrations © Sonia Holleyman 1996
The rights of Hiawyn Oram to be identified as the author and
of Sonia Holleyman to be identified as the illustrator of this work
have been asserted by them in accordance with the
Copyright, Designs and Patents Act, 1988.
A CIP catalogue record for this book is available from the British Library.
1 3 5 7 9 10 8 6 4 2
Printed in Great Britain

MONA the VAMPIRE

The Tinned Poltergeist

HIAWYN ORAM

ORCHARD BOOKS

Contents

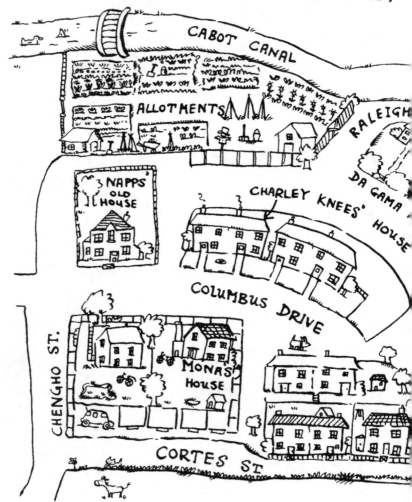

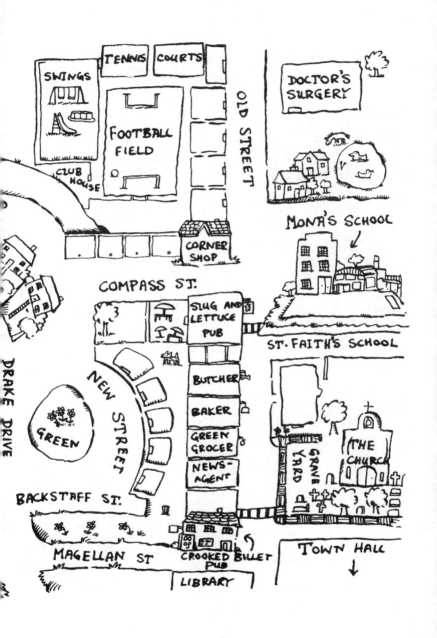

THE CAST

MONA

CHARLEY-KNEES
(ALIAS ZAPMAN)

FANG

POLTERGEIST

MUM

DAD

CHARLEY'S BIG BROTHER

TOM CHANCER

HEAD

Chapter 1
Something About

It was early Sunday morning. Everyone in Columbus Drive was fast asleep except Mona, Fang and Charley-Knees. Charley had crawled through the hedge at the back of Mona's garden and was throwing bits of gravel at Mona's window.

Mona opened the window a crack. "What is it?" she call-whispered.

"I was looking for you," Charley-Knees call-whispered back.

"What for?" called Mona.

"Because something's about."

Mona opened the window a little more. "Something like what?"

Charley-Knees looked round nervously. "Don't know exactly," he stammered, "except it moves things and makes people screech ..."

Mona was impressed. Moves Things and Makes People Screech sounded like a good way to start Sunday. She needed to find out more.

"OK, Charley-Knees. You go round the front and don't worry. I'll be down."

She pulled out her box of vampire things and set to work getting ready. If a Scary Screech Thing was about then so were Mona the Vampire and Fang the Vampire Cat – and whatever it was *it had better look out.*

Chapter 2
Definitely a Polterwhatever

By the time Mona was Mona the Vampire and Fang was Fang the Vampire Cat and they'd woken Mona's father to tell him where they'd be, Charley-Knees was riding his bike up and down Columbus Drive – as if the Thing-Mover was right on his tail.

Mona had to grab his handlebars and refuse to let him go until he calmed down. "It's OK, Charley. Fang and me are here. Now where did you see it?"

Charley kicked a pedal round. "I never actually saw it. But it keeps moving things. My dad's tools. Keys. Money. Important papers. Tin openers. My dad's passport. Everything. And everyone keeps blaming me. And screeching at me. Screeching and screeching."

15

Mona jiggled her elasticated spiders and bared her glow-in-the-sunlight fangs thoughtfully. "Then I know what it is," said Mona letting Charley go so suddenly he hit the dust. "It's a *Poltergeezer* ..."

"A Poltergeezer?" Charley gasped through a mouthful of Columbus Drive.

PolterGEIST, coughed Fang.

"Yes, Polterwhatever. They move things and make people screech. Usually vases and teapot lids," said Mona. "But they could do anything if they wanted ..."

"Anything?" Charley stood up slowly.

"Anything," said Mona getting carried away. "Even cars. Even houses ... I can virtually see it now. Moving that lamp

17

post. Can you?"

No, coughed Fang, *because a Poltergeist is invisible.*

"Well," said Mona, "you can see the things moving that it's moving so it's definitely there. So what I say, Charley-Knees, is we make a trap."

"A proper trap?" Charley's eyes shone. "To catch it? Once and for all? Do you think we could?"

"Sure," said Mona. "We'll do it right now. In our shed. There's lots of trap-making stuff in our shed."

"OK," said Charley. "Though I think I'd better go and get my Zapman things, just in case ..."

Chapter 3
Putting On The Lid

Charley-Knees – or Zapman as he now was – turned out to be just as good at making things as Mona the Vampire.

While Fang the Vampire Cat lay guard on the shed roof, they hammered and nailed, chipped and chiselled, bound and wound until, very soon, they had a extremely traplike trap.

"OK," said Charley. "Now, how *exactly* is it going to work?"

Just what I'd like to know. Fang scratched on the roof.

"I'll show you when we get it in our house," said Mona.

"Hey wait," Charley pushed up his mask in a panic. "What do you mean get it in your house. My house is where the polterthing is!"

"But my house is right here. And my mum and dad fight too!" Mona stamped. "And things keep moving in my house. Library books and things too. So it goes in my house or —" But here Mona stopped in her tracks. Fang was arching his back on the shed roof – and it wasn't at birds or too-close dogs. It wasn't at anything ... except a wind ... a

strange little wind that had got up from
nowhere ... and seemed to be blowing
around the shed ... blowing and swirling
and rattling things ...

Mona shivered. She was all goose-
bumps. "Oh, Charley!" she breathed. "I
think it's here. The polterthing ... I
mean really here. I can feel it ... and so
can Fang."

"OK!" said Charley/Zapman whipping out his Laser-Lightning Sword. "Then now's our chance. Pretend it's finished whirling round the shed. Pretend it's looking in the door..."

But Zapman wasn't listening. "And here it comes!" he cried. "Into the shed ... lifting leaves and moving nails ... right up to the trap and now it's peering into this bit ... and this bit's swinging over

and bopping it on its invisible head ...
and now it's fallen into the tin and now
watch this...!"

And with that Charley/Zapman
slammed on the lid of the paint tin and
threw himself on top of that, just to be
sure.

"We got it!" he cried. "We got it!"

"I think we really did," said Mona the Vampire looking more scared than scary. scary. "I mean really, *really* did!"

Chapter 4
Not Just a Brilliant Idea

"Well, I can't sit here for ever," said Charley. "What are we going to do with it now?"

Bury it, mewed Fang.

"We'll ask my dad," said Mona. "Come on."

Very carefully, they carried the tin into the house. Luckily, by this time, Mona's mother and father were up and having breakfast.

"The thing is," Mona explained, "it's a real poltergeething."

"Polter*geist*, Mona, poltergeist," said her mother, "from the German meaning noisy ghost."

"Exactly," said Charley. "And because it makes everyone else screech their heads off. Anyway we got it all right. It's in here."

"Then we'd better label the tin," said Mona's father. "We don't want anyone opening it and letting a real poltergeist out all over the place, do we?"

So Mona ran to get her pens. Her mother gave them some sticky labels. Her father agreed to help them with the wording. And, after only a bit of squabbling between Mona, Charley and Fang about who would do which writing, this is how their tin looked ...

Front label

Genuine
TINNED POLTERGEIST
Invisible but will
Move anything.
Lamposts, scissors
Even cars
OPEN AT Your
PERIL

Back label

BEWARE
This Scary-Thing
mover should
not be let out
EVER.
owners: Mona the
Vampire, Charley
(Zapman) and Fang
the Vampire cat.

And when they had admired their
work and read the labels out twenty
times, they had only one more thing to
decide: where was the best place to keep
a tinned poltergeist?

Mona thought her room – definitely. Charley-Knees thought his room – without question.

Fang just kept hissing, *Bury it.*

In the end, their squabble was settled by Charley's big brother who'd been sent to get Charley home.

"It's not an idea!" Mona was furious. "It's real!"

"Real is it? How come?"

"Because we caught it," said Charley. "In our polterthing trap so it can't keep moving things and making everyone screech at ME."

"All the more reason I should look after it for you," said Charley's brother mysteriously. "I'll keep it under lock and key. And then you'll know it's safe."

And although Fang kept hissing, *Don't trust him, bury it*, after a lot of humming and ha-ing, Mona and Charley agreed.

A week later, however, they were to find themselves wishing they hadn't!

Chapter 5
Shock, Horror and Betrayal

It was School Fair Saturday. Mona and Charley-Knees were going round together. As they went, Charley was telling Mona what a good job his brother was doing keeping the poltergeist.

"Nothing's moved," he said, "so he's not let it out. Not once. It's great. No one's screeching at me. Well, not for moving things anyway."

But there Mona stopped listening. She was pointing and gaping. Her ordinary hair was standing up like Mona the Vampire's hair. For beside Charley's mother's White Elephant and Mona's mother's Natural Remedy stall, Charley's big brother and his friends had set up a stall.

It was attracting a lot of attention - and it didn't take much to see why. Above the cloth-covered table was a huge banner saying ...

SCREEE....CCHY SCA.....RY THINGS
ONLY 50p EEE.....EEACH!

On the table were boxes and tins and bottles for sale – all brightly labelled. There was...

DROWNED SAILOR
(DRIPPING WITH SEAWEED)
GHOST

HOLLOW STARING EYES GHOST

50p

50p

BOTTLED VOODOO VAPOUR

TINNED VAMPIRE BREATH

BOTTLED WEREWOLF BARK

50p

GENUINE BOXED BIG BLACK PHANTOM

DANGER

PIG GHOST

PHANTOM RIDER OF RIDDON CROSS GHOST

50p

But none of these were what made Mona point and gape at the most. Right in the middle of the table on a raised bit, with its own sign saying ...

TO BE AUCTIONED
COMPLETELY REAL
AND FRESHLY TRAPPED

GENUINE TINNED JUICE INVISIBLE BUT LL MOVE ANYTHING ILPOSTS SEEN EN CARS FERM

↑ BEWARE!

DEAD MOUSE GHOST

SQUASHED BAT GHOST

... was her and Charley's tinned poltergeist in its original tin complete with original labels.

And as she pushed her way through the jostling crowd thrusting 50 pence pieces at Charley's brother and his friends, she was beside herself.

Great fat tears of betrayal welled in her throat. "He's stolen it!" was all she could shout. "He's stolen it. He's stolen it. And he's your brother, Charley, so you'd better do something quick ...!"

Chapter 6
Mona the Vampire Appears from Nowhere

But when Mona stopped yelling and turned to look at Charley-Knees, she was met by more betrayal. Charley was gone. He'd melted into the crowd like the Artful Dodger. Mona burst into tears and dashed for crying-cover under the table of her mother's stall. There she huddled between the baskets and boxes and let go on the sobbing. She sobbed so loudly that eventually her mother crawled in beside her.

"Mona! What is it?"

But with all the sobbing Mona couldn't explain. "Nnnnothing," she sobbed.

"Look. I'll just go and find someone to serve on the stall," said her mother. "Then I'll be back and I'll bring you a toffee apple!"

This comforting thought did the trick.

Mona's sobs began to subside. And through drier eyes she was able to see ... a corner of her vampire cloak and one of Fang's great green eyes, peering out of a basket.

"Oh thank goodness!" she cried. "I forgot I packed you. Oh thank goodness, thank goodness!"

And in no time at all – from under the table though as if from nowhere – stepped a terrifying sight: Mona the Vampire and Fang the Vampire Cat in Get-Back-our-Poltergeist mood!

Chapter 7
Moving White Elephants

"OH NO! WHERE DID YOU COME FROM?" Charley's brother yelped as they appeared at his elbow.

"Well, wherever it was, you can get back there," said one of his laughing friends. "And get that cat off our poltergeist tin. We're about to start the auction."

"No," said Mona the Vampire.

No, hissed Fang the Vampire Cat.

"Because it's not yours, it's ours," hissed Mona. "And we want it back. Now."

The crowd pressed closer.

"Hey, what's going on?" cried Tom Chancer, the biggest boy in the school. "And when's this auction starting?"

Charley's brother started to answer but Fang got in first.

He arched his back on the tin and began to caterwaul..

IT'S NOT STARTING, NOT EVER. BECAUSE THIS IS A REAL POLTERGEIST. IT'S DANGEROUS AND IT'S NOT FOR SALE

... while Mona repeated everything he said just to make sure everyone heard.

"Real?" Tom Chancer burst out laughing. "There's no such thing as a real poltergeist!" And the crowd joined in. They roared with mocking laughter. Real poltergeist! What a joke!

Mona blushed to the colour of beetroot. Her heart pounded. She wanted to run. Everyone in the school seemed to be pointing at her. She was about to make another dash for under her mother's stall. But then she heard it...

... the voice of Charley-Knees – or rather the voice of Zapman.

He was standing by his mother's White

ITS REA

Elephant stall, waving his Laser Lightning sword. "Mona the Vampire's right!" he yelled. "The poltergeist is real. We trapped it. So we should know!"

And this was all Mona needed. Charley hadn't run out on her after all.

Her courage returned. "And if you don't believe us, then we'll show you!"

The crowd immediately stopped laughing.

"OK," said Tom. "Show us. Show us Little Miss Frightening Vampire. Open the tin and show!"

Are you crazy? Fang hissed.

But Mona couldn't stop now.

"All right!" she said, pushing Fang off the tin. "I will!"

An uneasy hush fell.

"Er ... look ..." Charley's brother broke in. "This stall is just for fun. Like selling Scotch Mist and Mountain Air. And half our takings are for the school anyway. Still, if it matters so much, take your polter ..."

But his words came too late.

Mona was already pulling off the sticky tape and prizing off the lid.

For a moment nothing happened.

Tom coughed as if to say, 'See, nothing there ...'

But then there was a soft sigh which became a flutter ... which became a small gust ... which turned into a whoosh ... over the White Elephant Stall.

Then a vase flew into the air.

So did a pot and a pan.

So did a pair of brass tongs.

So did a brown teapot.

The crowd shivered. There were a few squeals. Then everyone started screaming, "It is real! It's a real poltergeist! RUUUUU....NNN!"

And they ran in all directions. Still screaming their heads off. Even Charley's brother and big brave Tom Chancer.

Chapter 8
Explaining the Unexplainable

Mona was something of a curiosity round the playground on the Monday after the fair. So was Charley-Knees. Even the Head sent a message to say she wanted to see them to discuss the matter.

"Now," she said, "I'd like you to tell me what really happened on Saturday ... from the beginning."

So, taking a deep breath, Mona did her
best.

"The problem is, Mona," said the Head when she'd finished, "I don't believe in ghosts or poltergeists. I think someone must have been under that White Elephant stall throwing things in to the air."

"Like who?" said Charley-Knees.

"Like you," said the Head.

"But Charley was standing on the stall. He couldn't have. Or everyone would have seen," said Mona.

"Well, someone else," said the Head. "Your ... mother...?"

"My mother?" Mona was horrified in case it had been. But then she remembered ...

"And anyway," said Charley-Knees, "we know it's real because since it escaped, things have started moving again in our house. And I'm being screeched at again."

"Hmmm," said the Head, seeing them to the door. "I suppose it's just possible there are things that can never be

59

explained. All I can say is, if you ever catch another poltergeist, don't bring it anywhere near this school. Do you understand?"

"Yes, Miss!" said Mona and Charley.

Then they tore back to the playground to continue to be surrounded by everybody wanting to know about trapping poltergeists ...

And once again Mona did her best to explain the unexplainable.

"You feel it," she said, thinking of Fang and what he'd say in the situation. "You sort of put your head on one side like this and feel it. Though if you're a cat ... you just sniff ..."

You can feel it!

And that afternoon Mona the Vampire, Fang the Vampire Cat and Zapman got out their trap and followed their own advice.

Though whether they re-caught the first poltergeist or caught another one and what happened if they did, is quite another story.

MONA the VAMPIRE

HIAWYN ORAM * SONIA HOLLEYMAN

COLLECT ALL THE FANGTASTIC MONA THE VAMPIRE STORIES:

MONA the VAMPIRE	The Hairy Hands	1 84362 816 3
MONA the VAMPIRE	The Big Brown Bap Monster	1 84362 815 5
MONA the VAMPIRE	The Tinned Poltergeist	1 84362 814 7
MONA the VAMPIRE	The Jackpot Disaster	1 84362 817 1

 All priced at £3.99

Mona the Vampire titles are available from all good book shops, or can be ordered direct from the publisher: Orchard Books, PO BOX 29, Douglas IM99 1BQ
Credit card orders please telephone 01624 836000
or fax 01624 837033 or visit our Internet site: www.wattspub.co.uk
or e-mail: bookshop@enterprise.net for details.

To order please quote title, author and ISBN and your full name and address.
Cheques and postal orders should be made payable to 'Bookpost plc.'
Postage and packing is FREE within the UK
(overseas customers should add £1.00 per book).
Prices and availability are subject to change.